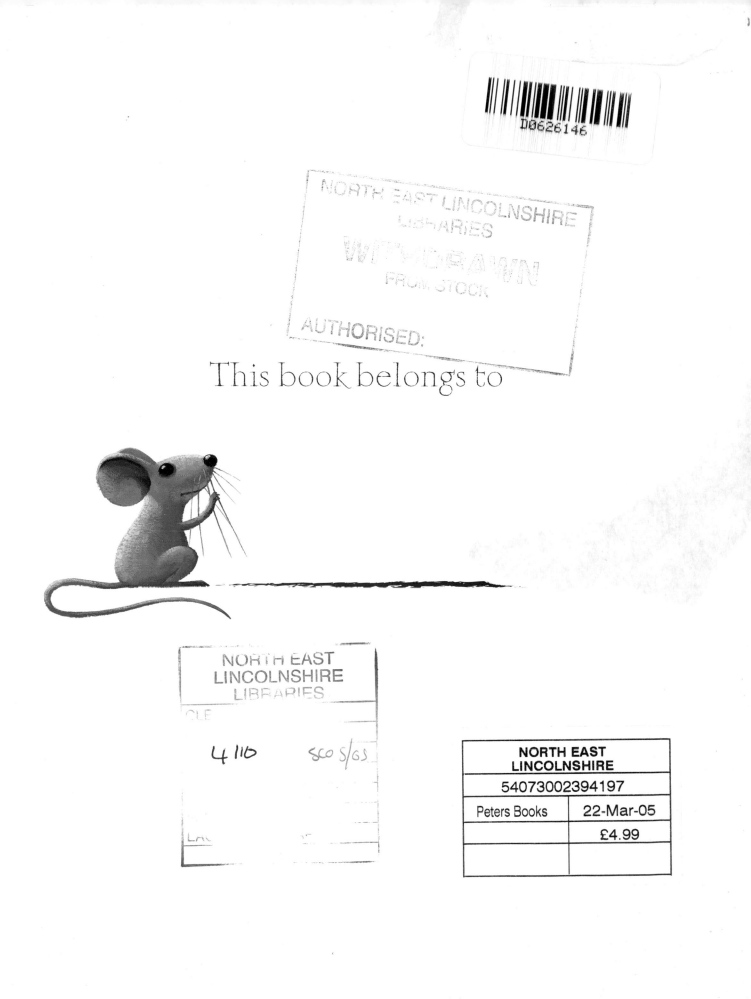

This book belongs to

For my boys -
Nathan, Calloway, and Rubén

Jon Berkeley

Chopsticks

OXFORD

UNIVERSITY PRESS

In a busy harbour, in the faraway island of Hong Kong, there is a floating Chinese restaurant.

It is built on a big barge, and has three storeys and hundreds of windows, and a roof of green tiles.

Every night people come in sampans to eat pork and fish and prawns and rice with chopsticks, and to drink green tea from china bowls.

In this floating restaurant lives a small
grey mouse called Chopsticks.

Chopsticks comes out at night, when all the
people have gone home and moonbeams
slant through the windows. He scurries
about looking for scraps of food
that the cleaners
have missed.

At the entrance to the restaurant stand two enormous pillars. They are painted in red and gold, and around each one coils a magnificent carved dragon.

One New Year's night, as Chopsticks washed his whiskers in the silvery light of a full moon, one of the wooden dragons cleared his throat and whispered down to him, saying, 'Little mouse … little mouse … climb up here so I can speak to you.'

Chopsticks looked up at the whispering dragon. He took a deep breath, and hopped onto the dragon's tail. Around and around the enormous pillar he climbed. Halfway up to the dragon's head he stopped. 'This is close enough,' he said.

The dragon sighed. 'I won't eat you, little mouse,' he said. 'I've been here for a long, long time, and I've never moved an inch.'

'Of course you haven't,' said Chopsticks.
'You are made of wood and lacquer.'

'That is true,' said the dragon. 'But, oh, how
I would love to fly. Up over the roof I would
go, and over the mountains, over the shining
cities and the dark forests. If you could free
me, you could come with me, little mouse.'

'I have always wanted to see
the world,' said Chopsticks.
'But how could I free you
from the pillar?'

'Only Old Fu knows how to
give life to a wooden dragon,'
said the dragon. 'It was Fu who
carved me and my brother here,
but that was many years ago,
and even then he was old
and almost blind.'

Early the next morning Chopsticks hitched a ride to the woodcarvers' workshops on the other side of the harbour. There he found Old Fu living by himself on a small sampan.

'Old Fu,' he said, 'I am Chopsticks the mouse, and I have heard you know how to bring a wooden dragon to life.'

Old Fu chuckled. 'You have come from the smiling dragon on the floating restaurant,' he said. 'I always knew that one would want to fly. He was the last dragon I ever made, and the finest of them all.'

Old Fu played a short tune on a small wooden whistle. The song of a blackbird was in his tune, and the sound of the water sighing around the sampan. He played it over and over, until Chopsticks had learned it by heart.

'You take this whistle and keep it safe,' said Old Fu to Chopsticks. 'The tune will only work when the moon is full.'

On the night of the next full moon,
Chopsticks climbed the wooden
dragon and played Old Fu's tune for him.

The dragon stretched and shuddered,
and groaned and sighed, and slowly
unwound himself from the pillar.
Chopsticks climbed onto his
nose and held on tight to
the dragon's whiskers.

The whole night long they flew
over lands that you and I only dream of,
returning to the floating restaurant just as
the sun began to peep over the eastern horizon.

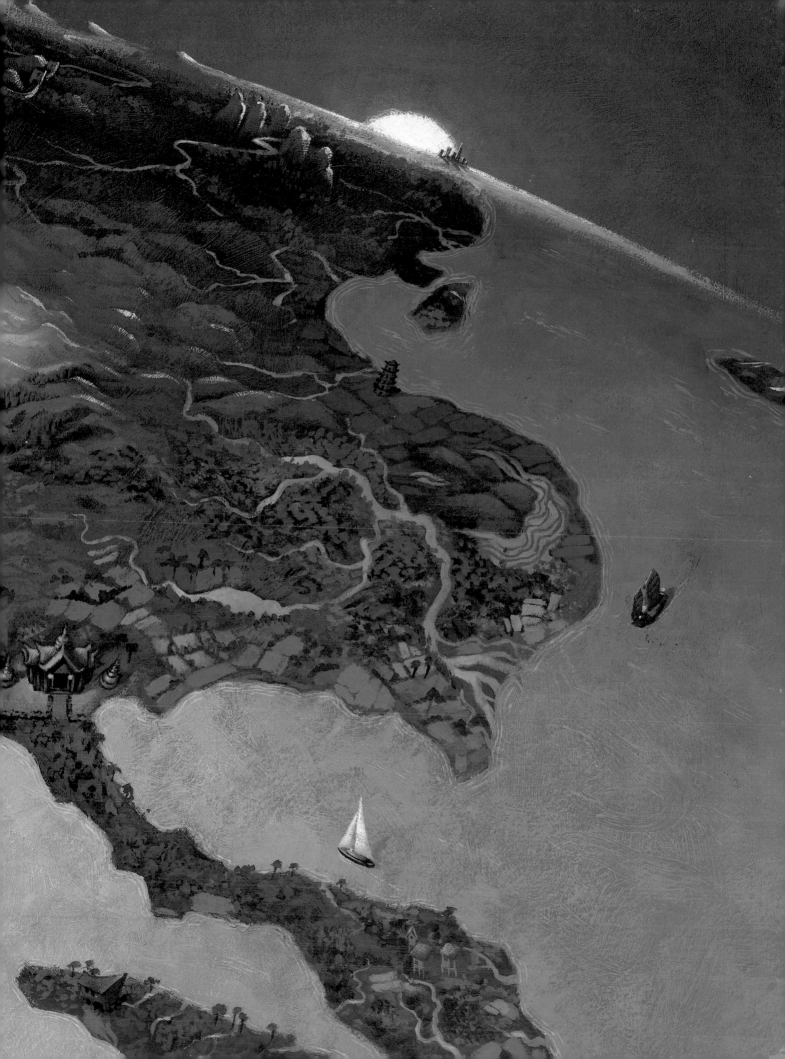

OXFORD
UNIVERSITY PRESS

Great Clarendon Street, Oxford OX2 6DP

Oxford is a registered trade mark of Oxford University Press
in the UK and in certain other countries

Text and Illustrations © Jon Berkeley 2005
The moral rights of the author/artist have been asserted
Database right Oxford University Press (maker)

First published in 2005

British Library Cataloguing in Publication Data available

ISBN 0-19-279062-5 Hardback
ISBN 0-19-272456-8 Paperback

1 3 5 7 9 10 8 6 4 2

Printed in China by Imago